For Naomi, Joe, Eddie,
Laura and Geraldine
M.R.

First published 1986 by
Walker Books Ltd
87 Vauxhall Walk
London SE11 5HJ

This edition published 2000

2 4 6 8 10 9 7 5 3 1

Text © 1986 Michael Rosen
Illustrations © 1986 Quentin Blake

This book has been typeset in Trump Mediæval.

Printed in Hong Kong

British Library Cataloguing in Publication Data
A catalogue record for this book is
available from the British Library.

ISBN 0-7445-7763-2

MICHAEL ROSEN
ILLUSTRATED BY
QUENTIN BLAKE

Under the Bed
The Bedtime Book

WALKER BOOKS
AND SUBSIDIARIES
LONDON • BOSTON • SYDNEY

Messing About

"Do you know what?"
said Jumping John.
"I had a bellyache
and now it's gone."

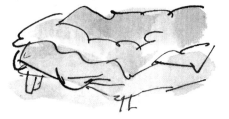

"Do you know what?"
said Kicking Kirsty.
"All this jumping
has made me thirsty."

"Do you know what?"
said Mad Mickey.
"I sat in some glue
and I feel all sticky."

"Do you know what?"
said Fat Fred.
"You can't see me,
I'm under the bed."

After Dark

Outside after dark
trains hum and traffic lights wink
after dark, after dark.

In here after dark
curtains shake and cupboards creak
after dark, after dark.

Under the covers after dark
I twiddle my toes and hug my pillow
after dark, after dark.

Things You Say

What If…

What if
my bed grew wings and I could fly away in my bed.
I would fly to the top of a high block of flats,
look out over all the streets
and then come floating slowly down to the ground.

I would fly to a misty island near Japan
and watch fishing boats cross the sea.

If my bed grew wings I would fly to a thick forest
where there was an old broken-down castle
that no one knew about, hidden in the trees.
And wherever I went
and whatever I saw,
all the time I was in my bed.

Things They Say

Nat and Anna

Anna was in her room.
Nat was outside the door.
Anna didn't want Nat to come in.

Nat said, "Anna? Anna? Can I come in?"
Anna said, "I'm not in."

Nat went away.
Anna was still in her room.
Nat came back.

Nat said, "How did you say you're not in?
You must be in if you said you're not in."
Anna said, "I'm not in."
Nat said, "I'm coming in to see if you're in."
Anna said, "You won't find me because I'm not in."
Nat said, "I'm coming in."

Nat went in.

Nat said, "There you are. You are in."

Anna said, "Nat, where are you?
Where are you, Nat?"
Nat said, "I'm here."

Anna said, "I can't see you, Nat. Where are you?"
Nat said, "I'm here. Look."
Anna said, "Sorry, Nat. I can't see you."
Nat said, "Here I am. I'm going to scream, Anna.
Then you'll see me."
Anna said, "Where are you, Nat?"
Nat said, *"Yaaaaaaaaaaaaaaaaaaa!"*
Anna said, "I can hear you, Nat. But I can't see you."
Nat said, "Right. I'm going out. Then you'll see me."

Nat went out.

Nat said, "Anna? Anna, can you see me now?"
Anna said, "No, of course I can't, you're outside."
Nat said, "Can I come in and see you then?"
Anna said, "But I'm not in."

Nat went away screaming.
He didn't come back.

These Two Children

There were these two children
and they were in bed and it was
time they were asleep.

But they were making a huge noise,
shouting, yelling and screaming.
"Look at me!" "Look at you!"
"Let's go mad!" "Yes, let's go mad!"

Their dad heard them and
he shouted up to them,
"Stop the noise! Stop the noise!
If you don't stop the noise, I'm
coming upstairs and I'll give
you a bit of real trouble."

Everything went quiet.

A few minutes later one of the
children called out,
"Dad, Dad, when you come up to give
us a bit of real trouble, can you bring
us up a drink of water as well?"

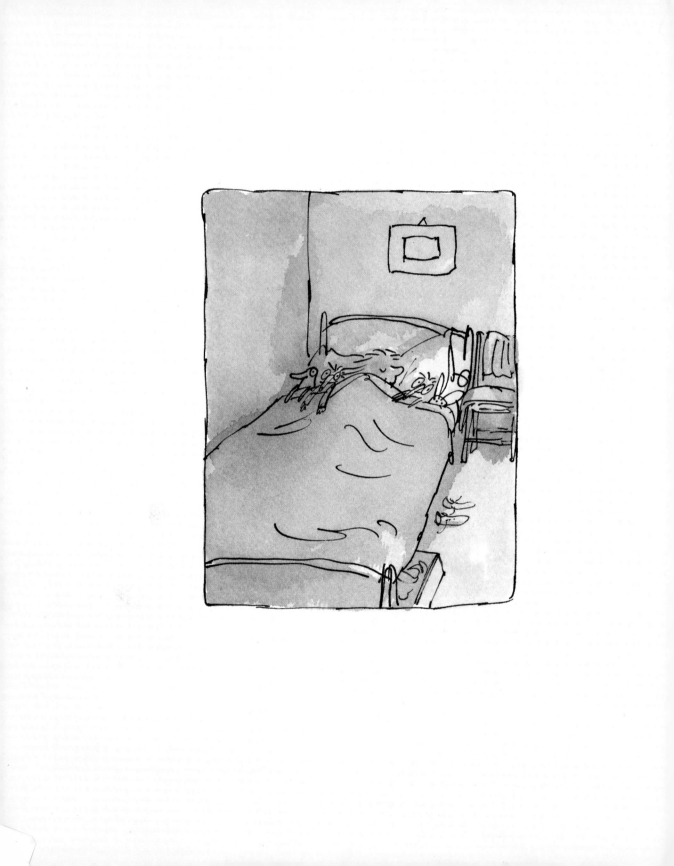

WALKER BOOKS

Under the Bed

MICHAEL ROSEN says, "What a clever fellow Quentin Blake is! I came to Walker Books one day and Quentin was sitting there with a scrappy piece of paper. On it was written a list of ideas: jokes, riddles, conversations, poems, things to do, cartoons … and that's how these books (pictured below) came about. When I was a kid one of my favourite books was *The News Chronicle I-Spy Annual*. It would last me the whole year. I hope my series does the same for kids today."

Michael Rosen is one of the most popular contemporary poets and authors of books for children. His titles include *We're Going on a Bear Hunt* (Winner of the Smarties Book Prize), *This Is Our House* and *Little Rabbit Foo Foo*. He also compiled *Classic Poetry: An Illustrated Collection*. He's a regular broadcaster on BBC Radio and in 1997 received the Eleanor Farjeon Award for services to children's literature. Michael Rosen lives with his family in London.

QUENTIN BLAKE says, "I have always liked Michael Rosen's poems; and what I particularly enjoy when I am illustrating them is that he seems to know everything about everyday life, but at the same time there is some fantasy that gets in as well."

Quentin Blake consistently tops all polls as the most popular children's book artist. The illustrator of numerous Roald Dahl titles and several Michael Rosen poetry collections, he has also created many acclaimed picture books of his own, including *Mr Magnolia* (Winner of the Kate Greenaway Medal), *The Green Ship* and *Zagazoo*. In 1999 he was appointed the first Children's Laureate. He lives in London.

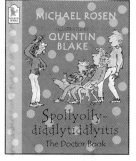

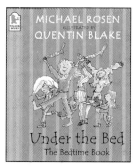

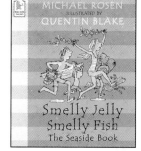

ISBN 0-7445-7764-0 (pb)   ISBN 0-7445-7765-9 (pb)   ISBN 0-7445-7763-2 (pb)   ISBN 0-7445-7766-7 (pb)